Angelique: Book Two

THE LONG WAY
HOME

CORA TAYLOR

Angelique: Book Two

THE LONG WAY HOME

CORA TAYLOR

PENGUIN
CANADA

PENGUIN CANADA

Published by the Penguin Group

Penguin Group (Canada), 10 Alcorn Avenue, Toronto, Ontario, Canada M4V 3B2
(a division of Pearson Penguin Canada Inc.)

Penguin Group (USA) Inc., 375 Hudson Street, New York, New York 10014, U.S.A.
Penguin Books Ltd, 80 Strand, London WC2R 0RL, England
Penguin Ireland, 25 St Stephen's Green, Dublin 2, Ireland (a division of Penguin Books Ltd)
Penguin Group (Australia), 250 Camberwell Road, Camberwell, Victoria 3124, Australia
(a division of Pearson Australia Group Pty Ltd)
Penguin Books India Pvt Ltd, 11 Community Centre, Panchsheel Park, New Delhi – 110 017, India
Penguin Group (NZ), Cnr Airborne and Rosedale Roads, Albany, Auckland, New Zealand
(a division of Pearson New Zealand Ltd)
Penguin Books (South Africa) (Pty) Ltd, 24 Sturdee Avenue, Rosebank, Johannesburg 2196, South Africa

Penguin Books Ltd, Registered Offices: 80 Strand, London WC2R 0RL, England

First published 2005

1 2 3 4 5 6 7 8 9 10   (WEB)

Canada Council   Conseil des Arts
for the Arts   du Canada

*We acknowledge the support of the Canada Council for the Arts which last
year invested $21.7 million in writing and publishing throughout Canada.*

*Nous remercions de son soutien le Conseil des Arts du Canada, qui a investi
21,7 millions de dollars l'an dernier dans les lettres et l'édition à travers le Canada.*

*Publisher's note: This book is a work of fiction. Names, characters, places, and incidents either
are the product of the author's imagination or are used fictitiously, and any resemblance
to actual persons living or dead, events, or locales is entirely coincidental.*

Manufactured in Canada.

LIBRARY AND ARCHIVES CANADA CATALOGUING IN PUBLICATION

Taylor, Cora, 1936-
Angelique : the long way home / Cora Taylor.

(Our Canadian girl)
"Angelique: Book Two".
Includes bibliographical references.
ISBN 0-14-301463-3

1. Métis—Juvenile literature. I. Title. II. Title: Long way home. III. Series.

PS8589.A883A845 2005   jC813'.54   C2004-905411-2

Visit the Penguin Group (Canada) website at **www.penguin.ca**

To

Metis children everywhere
and especially to my friends and family

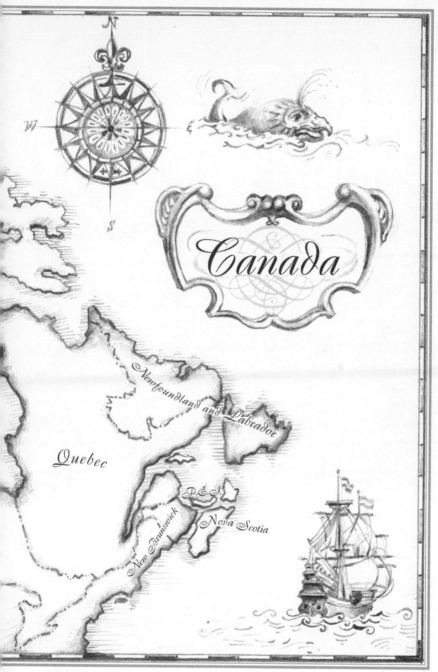

Canada

Quebec

Newfoundland and Labrador

New Brunswick

P.E.I.

Nova Scotia

 Marks the location of the story

CHASING MICHIF

I N THE LATE 1860s and early 1870s, the Metis who lived on the prairies west of Manitoba gradually began to change their way of life from one of hunting and trading to one of settling on farms. The Metis had previously spent summers following the herds of prairie bison and winters settling into villages such as Tail Creek and Buffalo Lake in Alberta or Petit Ville and Saint-Laurent in Saskatchewan. Now, the Metis began to settle in small farming communities. Farming, though, remained a secondary occupation; the main economy was still based on the hunt, and many men worked as guides and freighters, hauling supplies between the forts for fur traders such as the Hudson's Bay Company and the North West Company. The Metis men's endurance and knowledge of the country made them invaluable.

Angelique's family was part of this new settlement, although as long as there were buffalo to hunt, they would cling to the freedom of that independent lifestyle. In the 1870s, the little communities of Batoche and Saint-Laurent grew as more families moved to them from the Red River Colony in Manitoba.

Although there were villages and some basic farms, riches on the prairie continued to be measured a great deal by the possession of horses, just as they had been for Native tribes in the eighteenth century. Raiding horses from other tribes was a way of increasing wealth, and during their hunts, the Metis had to protect their stock. The most valuable horses, indeed frequently the most valuable property of any kind, were trained buffalo runners. These horses were essential to the success of the buffalo hunt and therefore an important factor in providing food for families and trade goods such as pemmican and hides.

The Native tribes and the early settlers had different attitudes toward property, and this difference created problems. To the Native people, horses were there for the taking. They were not for sale. If a man wanted a new horse, all he had to do was take one from another camp. The settlers regarded this as horse stealing, an idea that was alien to the Native people. The members of the early North West Mounted Police had to deal with these differences, but they found that they could do little about the Sioux, who crossed back and forth across the Medicine Line (the U.S. border) to steal horses (see *Sitting Bull in Canada*).

The raid that Angelique's family experienced was typical for that time. Speed for the raiders was most important; they had to drive the stolen horses as far as they could as fast as they could. Once the raiders had returned to their own territory, they were not likely to be caught.

AUTHOR'S NOTE

Some phrases written in Michif are included in this book. Single words are often translated right in the story, but for longer sentences, you will find the translations at the end of the book, in a section called Notes (page 105).

Angelique couldn't believe it! Not only was Joseph's pony not dawdling, he was galloping. She clung to her younger brother's back as they began to outdistance the screeching Red River carts. The carts were moving even more slowly than usual, carrying their loads of buffalo hides and pemmican. The hunters and their families were starting the long, slow journey home. It had taken the people from Batoche three days to get here. It would take much longer to get back.

Nobody cared. There was a mood of celebration in the air, and it promised to be a perfect rairie day. Anyone who could was walking rather than riding in the carts. Someone had begun to sing.

"Les souliers mous ki-ka-kiskanaan," warbled Joseph. *"La viande pilee ki-ka-miichishunaan."* He had a clear, sweet voice, Angelique thought, almost as good as her own, though he often sang the wrong words to tease her. Today, though, he seemed to be right in the spirit of things, and she was glad. The morning could not have been more perfect.

Angelique ran through the list of good things to be thankful for one by one, like beads slipping through her fingers.

At the top of the list was that Papa was riding Michif. She could see them with some of the other hunters who were riding along a nearby ridge overlooking the carts. The hunters made sure that everyone was moving well and that there were no stragglers. Michif's beautiful white tail streamed in the wind. When he cantered, he showed no sign of having been gored by the buffalo.

Angelique had loved the pinto horse since he was a foal, even though she knew she could never ride him. Only a hunter could ride a buffalo runner. And Michif had proved to be everything Papa had hoped—until the injury. Everyone said that her good care had cured Michif. She smiled. No limp. He moved with his old, smooth gait.

She went back to her list. It had been a good hunt, and no one had been killed. Indeed, Marie's father, who had been thrown from his horse and trampled during the hunt, was well enough now to be driving his own cart loaded with pemmican.

Even riding with Joseph was a pleasure. His pony, Gurnuy, was behaving and so was Joseph. If this kept up, riding with her brother home to Batoche would be much more pleasant than riding in the dusty, noisy cart. Angelique loved camping and all the feasting and dancing—all the excitement of the hunt—but it would be nice to be back in the little log cabin that Papa had built last fall. It would be good to stay in one spot for a while. It would be good to have a home.

She glanced up at the sky, ready to add the perfect weather to her rosary of happy things. The wide blue sky stretched on for miles—as far as she could see. Except—were those black clouds lying just above the horizon? It was early for a prairie storm. The clouds usually rose in late afternoon, and then the downpour would begin. Heavy rain would be a bad thing. Their camp would be a sea of mud in no time. They wouldn't have a dry spot to set up their tipi. And tomorrow the track would be full of mud, making the carts move even more slowly—if they did not get stuck and stop altogether.

Suddenly she caught herself and pulled away from the gloomy thoughts. She could almost hear her mother's voice: "Angelique, *ma petite,* do not borrow sorrow!" With her strong imagination working most of the time, Angelique knew that she not only worried about things before they happened, but she also worried about things that weren't likely to happen at all.

She laughed softly. She had done it again! She had imagined the storm and the mud so vividly that she could almost taste the rain washing over her face and feel the mud sucking at her moccasined feet as she tried to walk through it.

The ominous ribbon of clouds seemed to diminish before her. The clouds could easily move and storm somewhere else. The men would camp early if they thought there was a storm coming. Everything would be all right.

"Angelique!" The pony was walking now as they climbed a hill, and Joseph was pointing to the right. She had been so intent on looking at the horizon that she had not noticed the group of riders now just disappearing.

"How long have they been there?" she whispered, even though it was unlikely that the strange men could hear her.

"I thought you would have seen them too," Joseph twisted around to stare at her. "Were you gathering clouds again?" Joseph used their mother's words for Angelique's daydreaming. It made her smile, for she really had been with the clouds.

Joseph turned and reined Gurnuy around. Angelique knew he was going to ride back to tell Papa and Monsieur Dumont what he had seen, but it annoyed her that he hadn't answered her question. The pony began to run stiffly down the rise with a kind of hopping motion. Angelique hung on. It reminded her of why they had named Joseph's mount Gurnuy. When the pony had been a foal, they'd laughed at its way of bouncing around on stiff legs when it played with the other young ones. "He's a frog!" their mother had said and the Michif name for frog had stuck.

Angelique remained quietly seated behind Joseph while he excitedly told Papa about the riders. "There were seven men," he reported, knowing he was the bearer of important news, "and they turned as soon as they saw me and rode away—fast!"

"Were they Cree or Sioux or some of our people?" Papa's question was really directed to Angelique. Because she was the oldest, he expected her to be able to tell what the strangers were by their dress. Luckily, she was saved from having to confess that she had been cloud-gathering and not seen the men at first. Joseph was not about to let her answer.

"They were too far away to make out their clothes, but I'm sure they were not Metis like us. Why would they ride away from us so fast if they were?"

At last, she could put in a word or two without telling a lie. "They *were* going very fast," she said, "as if they were trying to avoid us."

"Maybe," said Joseph, "when they saw us coming over the hill they thought we were a man. Angelique is getting tall, you know ..." he added with a grin, "for a ten-year-old."

Monsieur Dumont spoke at last. "I doubt that seven men would run from one ... even if he were a *very* tall man." He looked thoughtful and,

Angelique thought, a little worried. "More likely," he said, "they knew that we had camped nearby and had been watching us."

Papa nodded. "Not Cree then. They would have met with us and known we'd had a good hunt and would share some meat with them. The Sioux raiding parties come up from the Cypress Hills sometimes." He squinted, looking into the distance. "We must be extra careful guarding the horses tonight." He smiled at Joseph. "You did well, my son, to be watchful and bring us the news, but—" his face was stern and he looked at Angelique too, "don't ride so far ahead of us next time. Had the men been closer, they might have decided not to risk having you report back and taken you prisoner."

The warning was not missed. Angelique could feel Joseph's tremor of fear as he leaned closer. He was, after all, only six years old, although he rode like an expert.

Monsieur Dumont looked at Gurnuy now. "Yes, and those horse raiders would have yearned for a steed such as yours!" His face was still serious, but Angelique could see the corners of his eyes crinkle as he teased. *He is a kind man,* she thought. *He wants us to know the danger but not be terrified.*

She'd heard Monsieur Dumont called *"le grand Gabriel,"* but it was not because he was tall. He was a short man, although very broad in the shoulders. In fact, he'd been called that because he was respected and admired for his strength and bravery and for the way he looked out for others. He could certainly handle the matter of possible Sioux horse raiders.

Still, as they rode back to the slow-moving carts, Angelique wondered if she might be able to arrange to sleep with Michif tonight to protect him from being stolen.

No storm came that day. Angelique had checked the cloud line along the horizon from time to time, and it had remained the same— nothing but a dark streak in the distance. It had not seemed to come nearer as they moved toward it.

They camped late. The men had wanted to cover as much territory as they could. Even so, with the slow-moving carts, they had probably only covered thirty miles that day. It would surely take them more than three days to get home. Angelique didn't care. Joseph had agreed to let her ride with him again tomorrow. That was good.

She wished that girls were allowed to have their own ponies. She could ride well, but she'd had to learn by sharing with other girls who were riding their brothers' ponies. It wasn't fair that she had to wait for a turn to ride someone else's horse or to ask her little brother if she could ride with him. Still, she really didn't envy Joseph. Gurnuy was not her idea of a horse anyway—Michif was, but only Papa could ride him. Michif was a buffalo runner, the most valuable horse a Metis could own. Angelique might dream of riding Michif, but she knew better than to imagine it could come true.

Once the campfires were lit and the big iron pots of stewing buffalo meat were placed above the fires, there would be music and dancing. They had found an alkali lake to camp beside. The bitter-tasting water wasn't good for drinking but that didn't matter. It was good for washing off the dust of the day's travel. The horses had been watered earlier when they'd crossed a small stream, and everyone had filled jugs of water— enough for their own drinking and cooking.

As usual, while the women made the preparations for the meal, the men went about settling things for camp. The carts were placed in a circle with the valuable horses, the buffalo runners— fast horses like Michif—in the centre. The other horses and those who had been pulling the carts were tethered around the outside to give them a chance to pasture and rest.

As soon as she'd swallowed her last mouthful of supper, Angelique slipped away to look for her friend François. She had seen him only once or twice during the day. He'd been riding his own horse and had spent most of the day with a group of boys. She really wanted to punish him by not speaking to him for a while, but she needed him tonight. She had a plan.

"François," she whispered, when at last she'd managed to get her friend alone, "did you hear of the Sioux raiders we saw this morning?" She had no doubt that he had heard. News like that would be all over the camp in no time. She wondered a bit how seven men glimpsed only for a moment could now be definitely called Sioux—and horse raiders to boot.

François nodded. "I heard you were the one who saw them."

Angelique felt a little guilty. She would not have seen them at all if Joseph hadn't pointed them out to her, but she didn't correct François. She needed him to take her seriously. "Joseph and I were riding a bit ahead—"

François interrupted her with a grin. "Yes! And you got in trouble again for leaving the rest!" He was laughing at her. "You are a bad one, Angelique."

Part of her was pleased that he should think she was daring, but she didn't want him to think she was reckless. Besides, this wasn't a bit like the last time she'd been in trouble. That was when she'd mistakenly run toward the buffalo herd and become mixed up with a wounded cow buffalo. That had been bad. The cow had charged. Joseph had nearly been hurt, and their father had saved Angelique just in time. But Michif had been injured—gored by the buffalo's horn.

This time, the fact that she and Joseph had ridden ahead of the others had actually been a good thing—otherwise no one would know that horse raiders might be watching their camp. She decided to ignore François's comment. She needed him for her plan.

"The raiders won't come near us until everyone is asleep. Will you come with me in the night? I want to make sure Michif is safe."

"Angelique, they've doubled the guard for the horses on the outside of the ring of carts, and any thief would have to get by them without disturbing anyone." François was shaking his head, but he smiled kindly at her. "I know you worry about Michif, but he really couldn't be safer."

Deep down, Angelique knew that François was right, but she didn't care. Checking on her father's beautiful pinto buffalo runner had become something very important to her. Still, she didn't argue. All she could say was, "Please."

François shook his head at her determination but gave in. "Very well," he said. "It would be a bit of an adventure to see if we can spy on the horses without our own guards knowing, wouldn't it?"

Angelique tried to contain her gratitude and excitement, but her smile was big enough to light the night. "Thank you, François," she whispered. "Shall we meet when we hear the coyotes howl?"

She knew the coyote packs would be gathering to feast on the remains of the fallen buffalo from their hunt. For the last few nights, the coyotes' mournful songs had filled the air. She loved the sound, except it aroused the barking of camp dogs, and then the shouts of *"kipaha kituun, kushon-d-shyin!"* would begin. Sometimes the men would storm out of the tipis, and that would not be good when Angelique and François were sneaking to check on Michif. But, she thought, perhaps that would just add to François's idea of adventure.

"Good." He was smiling again. "That will be late enough. I will meet you behind the north row of carts."

That night, Angelique lay awake, pinching herself whenever she felt her eyelids growing heavy. Mostly she kept herself awake by imagining the seven men she had seen that morning lurking somewhere outside of camp, moving stealthily toward the horses. In her mind she could see them circling around the other horses with only one goal—to steal her beloved Michif.

Nearby, she could hear that her parents were asleep at last. It had seemed to take forever for them to stop the quiet talking they'd been doing when they had first come into the tipi. Joseph, sleeping nearby, had dropped off almost the minute he and Angelique had gone to bed. He was no problem.

At last. The first coyote howl rose in the night sky. Soon there was a reply, then another, and another. It was time.

Angelique held her breath and slipped quietly out of her blanket, away from Joseph. Lying flat, she wormed her way toward the side of the tipi. She'd taken the precaution earlier of loosening the far side enough so that she could slip underneath. That way anyone watching the front entrance would not notice her leaving.

Now she slipped silently through the shadows toward the carts. The campfires had died down, and the coals had been banked with ashes in the hope that there would be embers to start the fires again at breakfast. There was no moon, but Angelique could see stars gleaming above, so close that it seemed she could touch them. She was nearly there. No dog had barked, but then she almost stumbled on one. The Letendres' old dog just sniffed at her, and then, knowing

her familiar scent, flopped back down and slept
again.

She was almost there. Yes, there was a shadow
ahead, a shadow slipping from behind one of the
carts. François! He had kept his word and come
to meet her. He *was* a good friend.

Now they were far enough away from the tipis
and the sleeping people that they were in danger
of being noticed only by the guards on the outer
circle of the cart horses and children's ponies.

The yipping sound of a coyote came from very
close, and Angelique and François looked at each
other. Was it really a coyote or a signal from the
raiders?

Moving silently together, they slipped between
the carts. She would know Michif's pinto
splashes of white even by starlight now that her
eyes had adjusted to the darkness. She reached for
François's arm and her fingers tightened. There
were dozens of horses—some still, some moving
restlessly about—but she could see no sign of
Michif.

CHAPTER N° 3

It was all Angelique could do to stop herself from running among the horses to look for Michif, but François was holding his hand up, signalling her to wait.

"We will circle around slowly and check to make sure," he whispered. "There are too many horses to see clearly, and we don't want to get them excited."

Angelique let herself be led back into the shadow of the carts. Then she and François crept forward. At first, they tried crawling under the carts, but from there they could only see the bellies of the nearest horses.

"Come." Angelique gestured to François to follow and climbed up the huge wheel of the nearest cart. Making sure that nobody was in sight, she climbed onto the bundles of pemmican. That was much better; now she could see well.

She scanned the herd anxiously and was sure that Michif was not there. Even François shook his head, but he didn't give up. "Perhaps he was put in another circle of carts, those of the people from Fish Creek or Saint-Laurent."

It didn't seem likely to Angelique, but she followed François as he climbed down and headed for the other carts. Her heart was heavy—she didn't hold out much hope. Horses belonging to families from the same places were kept together. It was better for them to be with animals they were used to. That way, there was no fighting among the horses to see who was boss. Why would Michif have been put in a different place?

As she climbed down the wheel spokes, her skirt caught, and she had to let François go by until she could untangle herself. Luckily the heavy trade-goods cloth was as strong as iron and didn't tear. There would have been no hiding that from Maman, who would surely want to know how it had happened.

There was no sign of Michif. Where could he be? Should she go wake Papa? She didn't dare. If there was another explanation for Michif's disappearance, Papa would know that she'd been sneaking about the camp late at night, and she'd be in trouble again.

"Perhaps he's been tethered with the other horses and Gurnuy by mistake," François whispered. "Let's go check."

Angelique didn't think they'd find him there either. Why would Michif be out among the ordinary horses when there was danger of a raid? She knew François would know that too, but she was grateful to him for trying to help by holding out even a small shred of hope.

She caught up with François as he slipped between the outer rows of carts. Beyond lay the prairie and the tethered horses. Many had finished pasturing and were resting quietly.

Now the friends would have to be very quiet and careful, or the men who were standing guard on the horses would see the movement. If they thought Angelique and François were raiders, the guards might shoot.

Angelique looked over at François as they dropped to the ground under the last cart and began to worm their way forward. Now he has all the adventure he wanted, she thought. Grass tickled her nose, and she feared she would sneeze. Luckily, the yip of a coyote close by distracted her. She could see one of the guards rouse himself from the campfire and stand to investigate, turning in the direction of the sound.

At that same moment, movement among the horses on the other side caught her eye. Some of the horses seemed to have broken loose from the tethers. From where she was, Angelique could see someone crouching behind the horses. Now another guard was running toward the loose animals, but it was too late; the crouching person had sprung onto the back of one of the horses and kicked it into a gallop.

How many horses had been untied? At first, it had seemed that only three or four were milling about loose. Now it was obvious that at least a dozen were beginning to gallop after the first one. To add to the confusion, the horses that remained tied up were now rearing and breaking their tethers. And there among the galloping horses was one who stood out—running fast as his white tail streamed behind, the starlight making his patches gleam. Michif.

The guards were shouting to one another now and trying to calm the other horses.

"Why don't they fire their guns?" Angelique spoke aloud forgetting to whisper, but it didn't seem to matter with all the noise from the snorts of the horses and the shouts of the men. "That would bring out all the men to pursue the raiders."

François shook his head. "They'd never hit the raiders and might injure one of the horses. Once the camp is raised, they will send out a party to try to bring back the horses. And the shots would probably cause more of our horses to break loose and stampede after the others," he added in a satisfied way for having thought of it.

"But Michif will be far, far away by then!" There was a sob in Angelique's voice. She couldn't help it.

Then she realized François was slipping away, running low toward one of the horses still tethered. She scurried after him, wondering what he was up to and not about to let him out of her sight.

It wasn't until she saw him throw himself over the back of the horse and sit up that she realized it was his own pony. Pisiskees was a piebald pony, bigger than Gurnuy, as big as some of the smaller cart horses. He was white with a black mane and tail, and black rings around his eyes. No wonder François's grandmother had given him the Cree name for raccoon. Angelique thought his white-rimmed eyes made him look a little loco most of the time.

"Get the tether rope, Angelique, quick!"

Angelique tugged at the knot. Good. It had been tied properly, and she was able to undo it immediately. She handed it up to François who took it and then pulled her up behind him. She held on to François as Pisiskees broke into a trot and then a gallop.

Suddenly, she saw one of the guards raise his rifle. She was terrified. Of course he would think they were raiders too! And François was using part of the tether rope as a hackamore to steer the horse right toward the guard.

Then she realized what François was up to. If they got close enough to the man before he fired, he would recognize them. She could see who it was: Michel Dumas, her father's cousin, who was a neighbour in Batoche.

"Michel!" Angelique screamed, leaning as far out as she could from behind François. "No! Don't shoot!"

It worked. As they sped by, Michel lowered his gun and stood with a shocked look on his face. Angelique didn't dare look back. She and François flattened themselves on Pisiskees's back and hung on.

CHAPTER N.º 4

Angelique wasn't sure whether Pisiskees was running because of something François was doing, or because he thought he was part of the stampede of loose horses and was racing to catch up. Whatever the reason, he was certainly moving faster than she'd ever imagined he could go.

She wanted to look up and see what was ahead, but she was afraid to shift her position. Her face was pressed against the warmth of François's shirt, and she had her eyes squeezed shut, as if that would somehow keep her from falling from the speeding animal. Pisiskees shifted a bit, and Angelique realized that François had anticipated the movement, perhaps even caused it with the hackamore. The thought gave her courage to open her eyes and look, though what she could see of the darkened prairie grasses flashing beneath them almost made her shut her eyes again. At the speed they were going in the darkness, there was no way either Pisiskees or François could see well enough to avoid any holes. If Pisiskees were to step in a gopher or badger hole, it would surely break his leg, and they would be thrown.

She could hear François murmuring softly to his horse as he eased it from the headlong gallop into a trot and then a walk. "Slowly, slowly, *petit* Pisiskees." When they had slowed enough, Angelique sat straighter and could see that François was urging Pisiskees up a steep hill. "I think it will be safe enough to go to the top and see if we can get a look at which way they are going."

"If they are Sioux, they will be heading south, *non?* This morning Papa said something about them coming over from a camp in the Cypress Hills."

François didn't answer. They had reached the peak of the hill, and in the distance Angelique could see the horses, still running but being controlled by several riders who had herded them into a coulee. Soon they would disappear, although she knew that the men from their camp would have no trouble tracking them later.

Angelique felt heartsick. What had they done? This was much worse than sneaking around camp at night. She and François would be in trouble like never before. Besides, they were in danger out here alone. There might be other Sioux nearby waiting to see how many men would leave the Metis camp to chase after them. "Why don't our men come?" she asked, trying to keep the trembling out of her voice.

François shrugged. "I don't understand. Unless they think there may be a very large Sioux camp nearby and are preparing for that." He twisted around to look at her, and she recognized that he was over his need for adventure and was as frightened as she was.

Angelique was about to say they should go back, when the moon came out from behind the clouds on the horizon and bathed the prairie in silvery light. The scene seemed to change from night to day, although the moonlight gave things an eerie glow and made the rocks and bushes look like crouching animals or people. Now she could see the herd of horses disappearing ahead, and the moonlight caught a streaming white mane and tail. She changed her mind about going back.

"If we follow a ways, we can save the men tracking time and tell them where the raiders went," she said. There was more determination in her voice than she really felt.

She felt François's back straighten—he was in an adventurous mood again, she could tell. They began to ride carefully down the slope. Then François pulled Pisiskees to a stop.

"Do you hear someone coming? Perhaps it is the men from camp now," Angelique said.

They waited. The only sound was Pisiskees's heaving. Poor thing. Angelique realized they had ridden him very hard. It was good to rest him a bit.

Then she heard something. But it was not the sound of many horses, just one. A lone rider. That was strange. Perhaps it was one of the raiders who'd stayed behind to watch the camp. François backed Pisiskees deeper into the shadows, and they waited breathlessly. Whoever it was, he was following almost the same route as they had. If they were lucky, the rider would be intent on following his companions and would not see them.

Yes, the rider was following the gully, not coming up their hill, but there was something strange. Those were not the galloping hoof beats of a horse—they were more like something much lighter, something with a strange rhythm, something like…. She gasped when she recognized the animal galloping to their left. Gurnuy!

Oh, no! The stupid little thing had broken loose and was following the herd. And then she realized that it was even worse than that. There was a rider crouched on his back. Joseph had followed them!

"François!" she moaned. She wanted to cry. Why couldn't her silly brother have stayed put? He must have wakened and noticed her gone. Then in all the excitement in camp, he'd managed to slip through and get Gurnuy. At least he'd taken the time to put on the bridle. "François, we've got to stop him!"

François had already nudged Pisiskees into a trot, carefully moving down onto more even ground. Angelique and François leaned forward as the horse broke into a gallop, following Joseph and Gurnuy.

Pisiskees was much faster and was easily gaining on the pony, but Joseph was urging Gurnuy to run hard. He hadn't looked back and obviously thought he was being pursued by an enemy.

"Joseph!" Angelique risked a call. Not too loud. She wanted her voice to carry only as far as her brother, though the raiders were well out of sight and probably out of earshot by now.

They were almost upon him. Soon François could pull ahead, and Joseph would see who they were.

It was then that Gurnuy stumbled, and though he did not fall, his head went down with a jerk. Angelique wanted to cry out, but her voice caught in her throat. Joseph lost his grip and went flying over the pony's head. He landed with a sickening thud nearby and lay very still.

Angelique leapt off Pisiskees before François was able to stop him completely. She ran to her little brother and turned him over carefully. She was afraid his neck might be broken, but although he lay in a crumpled heap, his head seemed to be at a normal angle. Carefully, she felt for broken bones, the way she'd seen her father do when Joseph had fallen from his pony before.

François knelt beside Angelique, holding Pisiskees's rope. "I think he's just knocked out," he said quietly.

Carefully, Angelique felt for broken bones, the way she'd seen her father do when Joseph had fallen from his pony before.

Angelique tried to keep her voice calm. "Joseph! Joseph! Do you hear me?"

No response, although she could see that Joseph was breathing—taking gasping breaths.

"He's had the air knocked out of him," François said. He was having trouble holding onto Pisiskees, who was straining to leave. Angelique realized that the horse wanted to follow Gurnuy. She looked up. That wretched pony had not stayed by his fallen master as he'd been trained to do but had taken off after the other horses.

Joseph was moaning now and had opened his eyes. The shock of seeing his sister seemed to overcome any injuries. "Angelique! I thought you'd been kidnapped by the raiders. I was coming to save you."

Angelique was torn between a feeling of affection for her brave but foolhardy brother and exasperation that he'd added to their problems. Now there would be three riders on poor Pisiskees. Any chance of following the raiders was gone.

They would accomplish nothing but getting themselves into a great deal of trouble. There was nothing to do but head back to camp.

She had to hand it to Joseph, though. He was one tough kid. He took the hand François offered and pulled himself up. He was a bit wobbly but obviously none the worse for his fall.

Soon they were all mounted on Pisiskees's back. The extra weight was really not serious. The three of them would probably only equal Papa's weight. Joseph was squeezed in between Angelique and François. If her brother felt dizzy, she could hold him on the horse.

François was keeping Pisiskees to a walk now, partly because of the extra rider but, Angelique thought, mostly because none of them wanted to go back to the scolding that awaited them.

As if he knew what she was thinking, Joseph spoke up.

"I know you weren't supposed to be out here, Angelique. Maybe you could say that *you* followed *me!*"

That gave Angelique a glimmer of hope, all right. Instead of being in trouble for leaving camp, she and François would be heroes for rescuing Joseph.

François liked the idea, too. "That would be very good, Joseph," he said, "but you'll be in serious trouble for leaving camp. How are you going to explain that?"

Joseph thought a bit. "I could say that I went to see if Gurnuy was all right, and he ran away with me!"

His voice was excited and a bit smug for having come up with such a clever excuse, and Angelique hated to shoot holes in it. "But," she pointed out, "how will you explain that you had time to bridle him first?"

François groaned. "She's right. And there is the problem that Michel Dumas saw us as we rode out. What if someone saw you ride out *after* us? It will be hard to explain why we were pursuing you *before* you left camp!"

Angelique took a deep breath. She hated to see a wonderful excuse slip away. "I think," she said, "that we should stick to it anyway. People will have so much on their minds, they might not bother to check it out." She sighed. "Joseph's plan is our only hope."

Pisiskees was trotting now. Angelique wondered just how far they had come in their headlong gallop through the night. It might take quite awhile to get back. Surely some of the men from camp would be coming. They would not wait until morning to begin tracking. Even in this bad light, a herd of horses could be followed.

Then she heard the hoof beats. Not a single horse this time but several.

"Oh, François," she breathed, "at last! They are coming!"

"Yes," he agreed. "We'll meet them and tell them the direction to go. At least we'll have done something good."

"Besides rescuing me?" Joseph obviously liked the idea of being vital to the story.

Angelique gave him a little squeeze. This might

work out all right after all. "Yes," she said, "besides rescuing you!"

She had assumed that the first riders out would be Monsieur Dumont and Papa, but as the group came closer, she recognized neither the men nor the mounts. "Are these some of the Fish Creek people?" she whispered to François.

"Perhaps. There are probably men fanning out in several directions, hoping to learn where the horses went." He gave Pisiskees a swat with the end of the rope he held, urging the horse faster.

The moon had gone under a cloud, and it was difficult to see even as they came closer. The men were moving fast, coming directly toward them now.

Too late they realized these men were not from their camp. François tried to pull Pisiskees away, but without a bridle, he only managed to turn at an angle. The riders were upon them by then.

There were shouts in a language Angelique did not understand. Angry faces glared at her. And then she felt herself seized, a rough arm across her face as someone else pulled Joseph out of her arms. She heard him cry out and struggled to see where he was and answer him, but she could not see. She felt as if she were smothering, her nose smashed against the buckskin sleeve. Then she was flung across the smelly saddle blanket of one of the riders. Their capture had taken no time at all. The horses were now galloping after the other raiders. Her heart sank. She knew that this was worse than any of the other events of the night.

And it was just the beginning.

CHAPTER N° 6

Lying on her stomach across the galloping horse, Angelique felt as if the breath were being pounded out of her with every movement. She worried about Joseph. If he was in the same position as she was, it could be very bad—especially after his fall. She tried to twist her neck to see him, but she was facing away from the other horses. All she could do was try to shift herself so that the pounding was not so bad and close her eyes. And pray.

The men were shouting to each other, but Angelique didn't understand a word.

The moon had come out again. Since she couldn't see the other riders, she lifted her head and tried to see over the rider's leg. *Please, let there be someone coming. Please ...*

The riders seemed to be increasing their speed, if that was possible. Of course, with the moon so bright, they would be easily seen from a great distance if they did not make it to the coulee where the Metis horses had been taken.

Angelique could see glimpses behind her before the movement of the horse made her head thump against its back. It hurt and she knew she couldn't keep moving her head like that for very long. Without meaning to, she moaned. The man who'd taken her must have heard her, and he reached back and grabbed her. For a moment, as she dangled alongside the speeding horse, she feared the man intended to drop her beneath the hooves. But no, his hold was sure and strong. He was pulling her up to sit in front of him.

He growled threateningly in her ear, words that meant nothing to her, except she knew they were a warning to be still. She was bouncing so much that she was afraid she would fall off. She grabbed a handful of mane. Better to be in trouble for that than to fall and risk being trampled.

Now she could see the other riders. There were three, each with a prisoner. She was grateful that the others were sitting upright. Joseph seemed to be doing all right. By the look on his face, the thrill of the wild ride had overcome some of his fear. François, on the other hand, looked grimly unhappy. She wanted to catch his eye but couldn't. He was trying to keep watch on Pisiskees galloping alongside. The poor piebald pony, already labouring to keep up, was falling behind, pulled along by the tether rope held by one of the raiders.

Angelique was much more comfortable now, but getting a glimpse of anyone following was hopeless. She could see something ahead. A horse standing, looking back at them. A horse with no rider. Of course! They'd caught up to Gurnuy.

She could see Joseph's face brighten in the moonlight. He did love that stupid pony of his.

The man Angelique was with pulled his horse over to the pony to catch the reins, but at the last minute, Gurnuy sprang away and began to gallop out of reach. She was sure that her rider could have run the pony down, but he just swung his horse back and continued onward. She was able to twist herself enough to see that Joseph's pony was now following slowly along.

They were almost at the coulee now. The men were speaking again, probably about where their companions had gone. They would know, she supposed. It would have been planned before the raid. Were there only four men with the stolen horses? Together with these three they would make up the seven men that she and Joseph had seen that morning. She hoped that were true, but she feared it was not. How many more were there?

Once into the coulee, they would not be seen. Now the riders were slowing. The one pulling Pisiskees had let go of the tether. Just in time too, poor thing; he was slowing a lot, falling back almost to be with Gurnuy. The two ponies would probably follow now anyway, and the raiders would want them. Ponies were useful, although they had nothing like the value of a buffalo runner like Michif. Still, Angelique knew, any horses were riches to the plains people.

Her body was aching from the rough ride. She worried again about Joseph, but he seemed to be faring well. It felt like hours later when they finally stopped. Angelique had no idea how much time had passed, but she realized that the prairie was brightening with the eerie pre-dawn light. It would be a long while until sunrise.

It appeared the raiders had a plan, and the horses had to be rested. She was lifted and dropped unceremoniously to the ground. She caught herself before she fell, although her legs were wobbly. She stumbled over to try to catch Joseph when he was pushed from the horse, but François beat her to him.

"Poor Joseph!" she crooned. All her frustration at him for his venturing out was washed away. If she felt any anger at all, it was with herself for not having stayed in bed. Although each time she thought of Michif, she doubted she would have changed anything at all.

Joseph ignored her. He looked shaken and scared, but all he said was, "Gurnuy got lost."

It was true. They hadn't seen any sign of the two ponies for a long time.

François looked sad, too. "They might have given up and headed back to camp," he said, but his voice didn't have much hope in it. "It would be good if they were found … people would know to come look for us in this direction."

All too soon, the men were getting ready to ride again, and Angelique was once more on the horse.

How long they rode this time Angelique had no idea. Her throat was parched, and she was stiff and sore from the jolting ride. She squirmed in misery. She was sure all the skin on her legs had been rubbed off by the rough saddle blanket she was sitting on.

The sun seemed to have been up for hours when the men came to a stream and began to follow it. Angelique looked down thirstily at the clear running water and tried not to think of how it would taste. The stream would be bad for the trackers. No tracks would show on the rocky bottom, or those that did would soon be washed away. The stream disappeared into some trees with steep banks on both sides. A ravine. Then, as they followed the stream, a hidden valley opened up before them. There were the other raiders and the herd of stolen horses pasturing in the lush grass. Tears came to Angelique's eyes. Feeding with the others was her beloved Michif.

CHAPTER N.º 7

Once again, Angelique was pushed off the horse. She was ready this time and landed firmly on her feet. She allowed herself to turn and glare at her captor. It was the first time she'd really seen his face. Definitely not Cree or Metis. She couldn't remember whether she'd seen Sioux before. Probably not. They never came to Fort Carlton where Angelique's family traded, and even this hunting area was very far north for them. Like the Blackfoot, the Sioux would come into Cree territory only to raid horses, and then they would quickly retreat again. She went over and stood by Joseph and François. She was determined not to be separated from them.

In the bright sunlight, she could see the other men as well. And yes, there were only four more, unless there were others hidden somewhere. Somehow, she doubted that. The fact that there were only the seven men made her feel better, although she wasn't sure if it made any difference. The three Metis children were still helpless. They had no hope of escaping.

One of the men rose from the small campfire they'd been waiting beside. He pointed at François, Joseph, and Angelique and shouted at the men who'd brought them. Although she couldn't understand what he said, she was sure it was because of the trouble having them along would cause. Horses were one thing to steal; children were quite another matter.

François evidently agreed. "They've decided taking us was a big mistake." He nodded toward their kidnappers. The three men had given up arguing and were looking worried. "Perhaps they had planned to camp here out of sight tonight and trust that our people wouldn't find this place."

Joseph's brown eyes seemed to be melting into tears. "They will come for us, won't they, Angelique? Papa could find us here, couldn't he?" For the first time he seemed like the six-year-old he really was. She patted him on the back, nodding, but she said nothing. They must not let the raiders see that they were afraid.

Even François had lost his brave, adventurous look. If it weren't for Michif, Angelique might have felt hopeless, too. She comforted herself that one part of the quest had been successful—they had found Michif. She gazed toward him and couldn't believe her eyes. The pinto looked up and tossed his head. It was just the way he used to greet Angelique when she came to take him for a run while he was recovering from his wound. Would he come if she called him? She wondered. The possibility made a bubble of joy rise in her chest. It was all she could do not to try it just then.

"Michif!" she whispered. It was a promise. She would try at a better time.

François had been watching the men. "I think they are going to rest now and travel later, maybe tonight when it is dark. They probably don't want to risk being seen by anyone."

"Especially not Papa!" Joseph said.

Angelique was glad to see some of Joseph's old spirit back, but an instant later, he turned to her, and his face crumpled. "I need a drink, Angelique!" he whimpered.

"Oh, Joseph," she sighed, "I have a terrible thirst, too." She realized that she could ignore her own need, but she was prepared to fight for Joseph. She turned to the nearest of the men. *"Ostesimaw,"* she called. She hoped he wouldn't be upset that she'd called him a Cree brother. She didn't try any more words but just pointed to the stream and then to her mouth.

The man said nothing, only nodded and pointed for her to go and drink. She tried to take Joseph's hand, but he needed no urging. He ran ahead and threw himself down on a flat stone by the stream so that his face hung just above the water. He scooped the water into his mouth. Angelique and François were right behind him.

Angelique decided that the sparkling, dancing water was the best she had ever tasted. She felt like drinking the stream dry. Then she realized that would be bad and reached over to pull Joseph away.

"Not too much too fast," she gasped.

Joseph looked puzzled. "Can people founder like horses?" he asked. "Would we bloat up and die too?"

François had raised his head. Now he got to his feet. "Let's not find out!" he laughed.

They stood for a minute looking expectantly toward their captors. Would they be tied up? Angelique wondered. It appeared not. One of the men seemed to be standing guard at their end of the ravine, although whether it was because of them or the stolen horses, she wasn't sure. The others had thrown down their saddle blankets in the shade and were obviously going to make up for having ridden all night.

"Come," said François. "I think if we don't do anything suspicious, they'll leave us alone." He led the way to a grassy spot beneath the trees. "This is a good place."

"No blankets," said Joseph, but he didn't really seem to care. He was soon lying with his head on his arm, his eyes shut.

"Mon pauvre." Angelique smiled, patting Joseph's back as she lay down beside him.

François chose a spot close by on the other side of Joseph. Angelique didn't mind. This left her closest to the horses. From where she lay, she could keep one eye on Michif as he pastured. Just seeing him made her happy enough to forget their hopeless situation. If it weren't for that, she thought, she could be quite content. The fresh-smelling grass against one cheek, a gentle breeze caressing the other, the murmur of the stream nearby, and Michif close to her were almost enough to make her happy. At least for a moment she could forget her aching body and her worried parents, and how much she missed them. Where was Papa? Had their men managed to track the raiders? Were they, even now, coming close? She knew that Papa would be as pleased as she was to see Michif.

She was tired, so very tired, and no matter how much she wanted to keep Michif in sight, her eyes just wouldn't stay open.

I must be dreaming, Angelique thought. Had she dreamt that she and Maman were at the Fort looking at the beautiful cloth? Something incredibly soft lay against her cheek. Was it the blue satin she had wanted for a blouse? But this wasn't satin. More like velvet … warm velvet. Brushing against her. No … nudging her. She sat up suddenly, bumping into Michif and making him jump back. He had pastured his way over to her. He did know her!

Angelique jumped up happily. "Oh, Michif!" she laughed, holding out her hands to stroke him. He butted her with his head, the way he'd done

*Something incredibly soft
lay against her cheek ... like
warm velvet nudging her.*

since he was a foal. Only sometimes now he almost knocked her over.

There were shouts as the raider who'd been guarding the horses came running over. He threw a rope around Michif's neck and began to pull him away. Angelique wanted to run after him, but she realized it would be better if she let him go for now. Had the man thought she was trying to get Michif to ride away? Was that even possible?

CHAPTER N.º 8

Until now, the thought hadn't occurred to Angelique. The rule that a buffalo runner must be ridden by only one rider—the one who rode in the hunt—was so strongly imprinted on her that she had never even considered the chance of escaping on Michif.

And yet, now that the idea had formed, she began to wonder.... Would Michif let her ride him? And if he did, would he be ruined forever as a buffalo runner—Papa's buffalo runner? She fell asleep again as the possibilities swirled in her mind.

She must have slept quite awhile. The sun was low in the sky, and the men were obviously preparing to travel. François had probably been right. They would travel all night, and that would take them a long, long way from rescue.

Joseph was still asleep, but François jumped up when one of the men came running over to them. He'd seen Michif with her earlier, and he knew what she was thinking.

"Angelique!" He was looking at her with a combination of surprise and respect. "You could probably do it now!" His voice was pitched low enough that the men would not hear.

"Do what?" Joseph was sitting up, rubbing his eyes sleepily. "What could she do?"

François ignored him. "Michif knows you better than anyone because of all the good care you gave him after he was gored by that buffalo." He really was excited now. "I'm sure he'd let you ride him. He's so fast he could outrun their horses. You could ride for help!"

The same thought had been going through Angelique's mind. Joseph had other ideas. He jumped up and yelled at her. "You can't! He won't be Papa's buffalo runner any more if you do! Don't even think about it!"

Angelique regretted all the lectures she'd given Joseph about buffalo runners. He'd evidently listened well. Now she would have to try to convince him when she was hardly convinced herself. Worse still, the anger in his voice had attracted the raiders' attention. Now the men began a discussion while staring at the three children. They were arguing and pointing.

"I think," said François softly, "they're wondering what to do with us."

"I don't care!" said Joseph, plopping himself down. "I'm not going with them. I'm staying right here until Papa comes!"

Angelique recognized Joseph's most stubborn look. When he got this way, there was no persuading him to do anything. It always worked with her, and once in a while even their parents gave in to it. But she doubted it would cause him anything but trouble with these horse raiders.

"Joseph," she pleaded, "don't get stubborn now. These men can hurt you if you don't obey." She felt tears coming at the thought of anything worse happening. "Please, just do what they want."

François had been watching the men. "You know," he said—Angelique couldn't tell whether that was fear in his voice or relief—"I think they are just going to leave us behind!"

Angelique looked. The men were mounting up and were already herding the horses toward the other end of the ravine.

"No horses, no food … oh, François," she tried to keep the despair out of her voice, "we don't even know where we are!"

Joseph had jumped up and was yelling at one of the men. "You! Stop that!"

All the raiders had moved away. Only the one who had the rope about Michif's neck was still near them. Angelique hadn't noticed what he was doing, but Joseph had. The man was putting a bridle on Michif. He was going to ride Michif instead of his own horse.

"Oh, no!" she groaned. That was worse than anything. Even if they got Michif back, he would have been ridden hard, and if anyone could ruin him as Papa's buffalo runner, this man could. She wanted to rush over and attack the Sioux, but François was holding her arm.

Before she could cry out, the man had swung himself up onto Michif's back. Nobody moved. Nobody but Michif.

The horse seemed to fly stiff-legged straight into the air. He came down bucking and twisting. The Sioux was obviously a good rider, but he only lasted a few moments. Luckily, he landed away from them.

"Michif!" Angelique called, running toward the snorting animal. He looked as if he would race after the other horses. "Michif! Come!"

The man was already on his feet again, moving quickly to grasp the bridle. Michif reared and he ducked back. Angelique was quite close now. "Michif!" she called again, her voice urgent.

And then the miracle happened. Michif came running to her. She grabbed the bridle, though even as she did, she knew that she couldn't make the leap to his back. He was so much taller than Gurnuy or Pisiskees, and the man was coming so fast. But then François was there holding out his hands for a step up, and a second later she was high atop the horse's back.

She was riding Michif.

CHAPTER N°9

Papa always said that a good buffalo runner seemed to read his rider's mind. Now Angelique's only thought was to get away from the Sioux who was trying to grab Michif's bridle.

She let out a whoop, the way she'd heard the men do when they were about to race a horse, and pulled Michif away. Michif did her one better. Without seeming to need her guidance, he headed for the stream and the way they had ridden into the ravine.

The ground was rough and stony; the horses had walked, not galloped, coming in, and she didn't

*A good buffalo runner seemed
to read his rider's mind.
Without needing her guidance,
Michif headed for the stream.*

want Michif hurting himself. All they had to do for now was outdistance the man running after them. She pulled on the reins to slow Michif's pace.

Angelique looked back. The raider was far enough behind, and once he was in the stream, he would have to slow down too. The other men were shouting and starting to come after her, but they were nearly at the other end of the ravine. It would take time for them to get to her, even on horseback.

She got a glimpse of François and Joseph. They were climbing the bank, almost hidden by the bushes already. She hoped they would be safe there. The good thing about this stream entry to the little valley was that the banks were high on both sides. The only way out was on the stream bed, and Michif knew what he was doing.

The man had gained a bit before he hit the water, but now his moccasins were slipping and sliding on the stones, and he was slowing too. But the three riders behind were moving fast, and they'd soon be in the stream. Angelique didn't know if they'd risk trying to trot their horses through the rocks. They would catch her if they did. But she wouldn't risk hurting Michif by urging him to go any faster.

Just before the trees shut the valley from view, she scanned the bank where she'd last seen François and Joseph. Gone! The riders were pulling up their horses to enter the stream. Good. They had not even looked for the boys. If Angelique could distract the men long enough, François would have time to get away and hide himself and Joseph. Maybe the raiders would forget them or not care to look for them when they returned. Then even if they recaptured her, someone would be free.

"*Vite, mon bon* Michif," she breathed.

There was still some distance to go before she reached the place where the raiders had entered the stream, although the banks were not so steep now. A glance back showed her that the three riders were gaining. Her heart sank. She and Michif would be recaptured before they even had a chance to run. If only …

Michif really could read her mind! She hadn't wanted to urge him up the bank in case it was still too steep and he slipped, but he scrambled out of the creek and onto the slope. He lunged to keep his footing, and it was all Angelique could do to hang on. She held onto his mane with one hand, letting the reins go slack in the other. She would give Michif his head. He knew what he was doing.

At last they were on more even ground. Michif needed no urging—he started galloping. As they turned to ride out onto the prairie, Angelique managed a look back. One of the horses had slipped trying to scramble up the bank as Michif had. He had thrown his rider and fallen, blocking the other horseman. But the first rider was coming faster now, galloping after them.

"Now, Michif!" she crooned. "Now you can run." She crouched along his neck. She had not used the reins at all, and she wouldn't now. Wherever Michif wanted to run was fine with her. All they had to do was outrun their pursuer.

Angelique knew that she should be afraid, but all she felt was the thrill of riding her beautiful Michif. There were tears streaming down her cheeks, but it wasn't the wind alone causing them.

She'd known that the horses she'd ridden before, ponies like Gurnuy or other children's horses like Pisiskees, were rough rides compared with the buffalo runners and other horses the men rode. But she wasn't prepared for this feeling. As Michif stretched out into a full gallop, Angelique decided that this was as close to flying as anyone could ever get. Only the angels, she thought, would know better. For a while, she was so lost in the pure joy of it that she forgot the pursuer and even the friend and the brother she'd left behind.

At last, as Michif slowed to climb a small hill, she allowed herself a look back. She almost laughed. The Sioux pursuing them was more than a quarter of a mile behind, and the two other men seemed mere dots. In her brief glimpse, it looked to her as if they were stopped and waiting for their companion to return.

For the first time, she tugged gently on the reins. *"Piiyaatak,* Michif. *Piiyaatak, mon buu."*

Obediently, Michif slowed to a walk. Angelique knew there was no need for Michif to risk running down the hill. Besides, he hadn't really been able to push himself since his wound had healed, and she didn't want to risk another injury. There was another higher hill ahead, and from it she would be able to see whether they were still being followed.

She let the horse canter when they were on the level ground. She was curious to see whether every gait was smooth. They were. Lovely. She was beaming.

From the top of the next hill, she could see that her pursuer had turned back. She held Michif to stand there. She wanted to be sure that the men had given up and were not planning to circle around. Not that she thought they would. They would have seen enough of Michif's speed to know that they could never catch him, and besides, their main goal would be to get away, farther south, with the other horses they had stolen.

She would have been completely happy were it not for the boys. Michif was safe. Whatever trouble she would be in for leaving would be lessened by that. Papa could not be too angry with her when he had his prize horse again. And even though she was alone on the prairie and starting to get very hungry and thirsty, she was sure that she and Michif would be found eventually if she just kept riding north. But the boys were another matter. They were on foot and still in danger from the Sioux raiders. If the men really tried, they could track the boys no matter how well François tried to hide them.

"We have to go back for François and Joseph," she murmured. She was talking to herself, but Michif nickered reassuringly and tossed his head as if agreeing. That made her smile.

"Yes, Michif, we will wait until the men disappear, and then we must ride back again." Her face clouded. "But if the men recapture the boys and take them … then I don't know…. Perhaps it would be better if we rode on. We might meet our own men. They would surely be following by now."

Angelique was beginning to feel afraid. What if she made the wrong decision? There might not be a search party. Then, if the raiders had not recaptured them, the boys would be wandering on foot. They would be hungry and thirsty too.

"Oh, Michif!" There were real tears now. "What do I do?"

Michif raised his head and whinnied toward the other side of the hill. There was an answering whinny.

Angelique had been so busy looking back to see where her pursuers were that she had not searched the land ahead. Now she looked. Two ponies—really a small horse and a pony—were pasturing on the prairie below them. Gurnuy and Pisiskees. Joseph and François would not have to walk home after all!

CHAPTER N° 10

Knowing she could take the boys' horses to them made her decision easier. Still, she would climb one more hill and scan as much country as she could, in case a party of men from the Metis camp was anywhere in sight.

Nothing. The prairie stretched wide and beautiful below her. She wished she could just stay there. Could anything be more perfect? Clouds drifted across the sky as the sun tinged everything with the gold, red, and purple of the coming prairie sunset. The breeze was warm on her face, and her beloved Michif was beneath her. She bent and pressed her face against his neck. She loved the sharp tang of his sweat, the clean horsey smell of him. She wanted to hold this moment forever.

But she had things to do, and a brother and a friend to rescue. She let Michif walk down to the other horses. Gurnuy nickered in greeting and came to meet them. Pisiskees stayed where he was, pulling mouthfuls of the rich prairie grass. His tether rope still trailed, the end frayed from being dragged so far.

Obviously, Angelique thought, the thing to do would be to lead Pisiskees. Gurnuy would certainly follow if she did. But she didn't want to dismount. Without François there to help, she was not sure that she could get back up on Michif's back. Could she get hold of the rope while on the horse? Each time she tried to ride close enough to grab it, Pisiskees would toss his head and move away. Six times it happened. Would she be here all evening? She was sure that if she were on foot, she could get the rope. It seemed as if she would have to jump down. She'd already looked all around in the hope that there was a stone or boulder large enough to use as a step up, but this place had only grass and a few rose bushes.

Then another miracle happened. Just as she went to reach for Pisiskees's rope for the seventh time, he pulled up short as he tried to move away. Angelique looked down. Michif's hoof was right on top of the rope. Pisiskees couldn't go anywhere. Angelique grabbed the rope. Either Michif was the smartest horse in the world, or it was a lucky accident. Angelique preferred to think it was a miracle. Perhaps not a big miracle. Perhaps no one but herself would think it one. But it was a nice little miracle, just for her.

She smiled. When Michif moved, so did Pisiskees, and with one horse being led and Gurnuy following, they set out. She let Michif walk at first so that they could get used to leading a horse. If Pisiskees got stubborn and pulled back, she would be dragged off Michif's back. She didn't want to risk that.

Soon, though, Michif began to trot down the slope, and Pisiskees followed. She had to hold Michif from going too fast. She was afraid that Pisiskees would remember being dragged along at a gallop the night before and rebel. So far so good. At this pace, even Gurnuy was keeping up.

Angelique could not believe how far she and Michif had come. It seemed as if they had covered a lot of country since she'd decided to turn back, but the distant line of trees that hid the stream and the valley she had come from seemed just as far away as ever.

The sun was setting now. She would have another hour or two before it got dark. Prairie twilight lasted a long time at this time of year.

They had slowed to a walk. Pisiskees was still cooperating, so she decided to risk trotting Michif again. Angelique wondered whether François and Joseph had found a safe hiding place. Would the men have been in such a hurry that they would not have looked for the boys? She hoped so. She tried not to think about the possibility that they had been recaptured. Surely the raiders would know that would definitely bring Metis revenge. Horses might be overlooked for now if the Sioux went back to the Cypress Hills or even made it down to Montana. But she knew that *le grand Gabriel,* Papa, and François's father, Monsieur LaVallée, would never stop searching until they found *les enfants.*

At last, in the fading light, they reached the stream. At least Angelique was sure that the raiders would be far away, since it had taken her so long to get back. She let the horses drink and then could wait no longer. She slid off Michif's back and took a drink herself.

She would worry about remounting in the morning. She was stiff and sore, and all she could do now was rest. In the morning, she would see whether she could track the boys. In the meantime, this was a good spot to stop. If her father and the others tracked the stolen horses to this place, they would find her. The drink had helped, but she was hungry—what she wouldn't give now for a handful of the pemmican she and Maman had made. Even if she couldn't stew it and make *rababou,* it would taste wonderful. She was so hungry.

Thinking of Maman, the warmth of her arms—and her food—made Angelique feel even more homesick. She distracted herself by making plans. She would tie Pisiskees to a tree nearby and trust that Michif and Gurnuy would stay close. Except—where was that stupid pony?

Gurnuy seemed to have disappeared. No, there he was heading up the stream into the trees that hid the ravine and valley.

Angelique didn't want to move another inch she was so tired, but maybe it was a good idea. That was the last place she'd seen the boys, and it was a good place to camp. But the only way to get there was through the stream. She couldn't get back onto Michif, so she'd have to wade and get her moccasins wet. She was angry. A plague on that silly pony of Joseph's.

I must be very tired, she thought. *I'm getting stupid. I can't get onto Michif's back just now, but I've got another horse that's not nearly so tall.* She mustered the last of her energy and threw herself up onto Pisiskees. Leading Michif, she began to follow the stream and Gurnuy.

At the first sight of the campfire, Angelique panicked. The raiders were still there! She could never outrun them riding Pisiskees. He wasn't wearing a bridle; she couldn't even turn him around to get away. Everything she'd done today would be undone.

Angelique didn't have time to think of what she might do. A shout almost stopped her heart.

Someone seated beside the campfire was up and running toward her.

"Gurnuy," Joseph yelled excitedly. "You found me!" He threw his arms around his pony. "Look François! Gurnuy came all this way alone to find me!"

François was up now and running too, but he was looking at Angelique, Pisiskees, and Michif. He came and grabbed Pisiskees's rope as Angelique slid off. "Yes!" he laughed, "and look who else he brought along!"

Angelique stood swaying dizzily. She was tired,

so very, very tired, but this was the best sight she could have hoped for. She laughed, too, seeing the look on Joseph's face when he finally turned from welcoming Gurnuy. He probably still believed that his silly pony had brought her back, she decided.

François had taken the other two horses to a tethering spot. Pisiskees would be tied for the night.

Angelique walked stiffly to the friendly light of the fire and flopped down. She couldn't believe her eyes. Roasting on a stick-spit beside a bed of coals was a rabbit. Her mouth watered at the sight.

"François ..." she started as he came toward her, "how ...?" Then she remembered. "The raiders?"

"The others left heading south while you and Michif were being chased," he began to explain.

Joseph wasn't about to be left out. He had pulled off his pony's bridle to let Gurnuy pasture in the bushes nearby. "We hid—François and I—way up the bank." Words tumbled out in his excitement. He couldn't speak quickly enough to tell his story.

"The Sioux were in a hurry to leave, I think," François put in. "They were afraid you'd bring help if the three men chasing you didn't catch you."

"They didn't even look for us." Joseph had caught his breath. "We thought the ones chasing you might when they came back, but they just hurried on down the valley to try to catch up to the others."

"We waited, in case they came back … staying well hidden," François added.

Angelique was interested in their story, but her eyes were fixed on the golden brown meat sizzling by the fire. She was famished. François laughed, reached over, and tore off a leg. He handed it to her. She risked burning her mouth by biting into its succulence. It was hot enough to slow her down, though, making her take dainty bites, but so tender and delicious that she really wanted to devour it all at once.

Joseph hadn't slowed. "Yes, we waited for hours. Nobody came and then we decided that you would be well away, and if you found help you'd bring them here."

Angelique licked her fingers and smiled. Joseph's using "we" didn't fool her. François had taken charge perfectly, and she smiled at him. "You did well," she said. If Joseph thought she was speaking to him, then that was fine with her.

"We used a lace from François's jacket to make a snare along a rabbit path I found." Joseph seemed a bit smug about that. "And François killed a grouse with a stick. We ate that first," he added ruefully.

Angelique was relieved that they'd already eaten something. She was on her second rabbit leg and had been worrying that she was eating more than her share. A rabbit wasn't much for three people, especially three hungry people.

Joseph wasn't finished. "François showed me how to wrap the grouse in mud and bake it, so when we broke the baked clay, the feathers and skin came off too," he said proudly. "It was very good." Joseph looked at her apologetically. "I'm sorry we didn't save some for you."

Angelique laughed. "You didn't know I was coming to your feast! Besides, this is delicious. You are very good cooks!"

They fell to finishing the meal. Between bites, Angelique explained about finding the boys' horses.

"Were there no signs of people looking for us?" François seemed puzzled. "They should have been able to track the horses by now."

Angelique shook her head. "I could see for a long way from that hill, and there was no one. There were heavy clouds to the north, though." At the time, she'd only been impressed by the sunset colours, but now she realized those might be the same clouds that had bothered her the day before. "Perhaps there was rain and the tracks were washed away." Even as she ventured this possibility, her spirits fell. She could see their fathers and Monsieur Dumont caught in a torrent of rain.

"Never mind," said François, licking his fingers. "Tomorrow we will ride north and try to find our way back to camp. Even if we miss our people, we are bound to run into someone."

Angelique saw that the boys had managed to make a good pile of dead branches from the trees along the ravine. Someone would have to wake up every hour or so and keep the fire going. François was throwing a few of the bigger pieces onto the fire now. Angelique couldn't wait to lie down and get some rest. The horses were already lying down together near where Pisiskees was tethered.

The night was warm, but already the grass was damp with dew. Near the fire, it was dry enough to lie on. "Come, Joseph. François and I will sleep on either side of you."

Twice in the night, Angelique felt cold enough to waken and put some wood on the fire. Once François beat her to it. By morning, the wood pile had dwindled to a few pieces.

Angelique rubbed her eyes and looked ruefully at the coals. *If we had anything to put it in, we could have boiled some water for tea,* she thought. She was sure she had noticed some of the plants her mother sometimes used—the leaves made good tea.

The boys awoke shortly after she did. She'd put the last of the wood on the fire just to have a cheerful blaze. They had nothing to eat and only cold water to drink, but no one complained.

Joseph was still showering Gurnuy with praise for having found him as he put the pony's bridle on and got ready to mount.

Angelique smiled at François and shook her head. "Gurnuy, the Rescue Pony!" she whispered.

François grinned back. "At least it gives him something to think about." He looked up at the sky. "He hasn't noticed the weather."

Neither had Angelique. She'd been busy splashing cold stream water on her face and trying to comb the grass and twigs out of her hair with her fingers. Now she looked up. True, the sun had come up, but there were clouds to the north. In fact, they would be riding straight toward the storm-darkened sky.

CHAPTER N⁰ 12

As they rode out into the open prairie, they felt the wind. *No wonder the sky filled with clouds so quickly,* Angelique thought.

"We'll have to keep the horses headed north," François called. "They'll want to head downwind."

Angelique nodded. François was right, of course. They must go north. Still, she wondered whether the horses weren't more sensible. Maybe they should just go back and take shelter from the rain. She could see François struggling to keep Pisiskees headed in the right direction. She and Joseph were lucky to have horses with bridles. That Sioux had done her a favour when he'd tried to ride Michif. She'd ended up with the bridle. She wasn't sure she could have ridden Michif without it, no matter how much he liked her.

By the time the rain hit, they were back to where she'd found the ponies the day before. At least, she thought she recognized the spot. The rain was cold. The drops were hard and stung her face. In no time, her blouse was soaked, and she was shivering. She wished they'd stayed back by the stream. At least there the trees would have given them a bit of protection.

She could see Joseph riding bravely on. He had his stubborn look on his face. This time she was glad of it. He wouldn't complain or quit as long as he felt that way.

As they crested the hill where she'd looked for rescuers a day ago, she reined over to François. He was having more trouble than ever trying to steer Pisiskees. The horse was tossing his head angrily, trying to shake the hackamore François had made by looping the tether rope around Pisiskees's nose.

François looked glad to see her. "Maybe we should give the horses their heads now," he called. "They'll probably find some shelter if we do."

Angelique nodded, rain streaming down her cheeks. "Good idea. I'll tell Joseph," she said, reining Michif after her brother and Gurnuy who were stolidly plodding on into the storm.

For a little while the three horses stood together seeming to wait for instructions, their riders waiting in turn for the horses to make a move. Finally, with a toss of his head, Pisiskees took the lead and headed west.

At least, Angelique thought, as she wiped the rain out of her eyes, *it's easier than facing into the storm.* The horses did not go far. They found a gully with a bit of overhanging bank. The three riders scrambled off their horses and huddled there, hoping the storm would pass, but fearing it was not going to anytime soon.

The three riders scrambled
off their horses and huddled
in the gully beneath a bit
of overhanging bank.

CHAPTER No. 13

The bank they were sheltering in was sandy. François began to scoop out the loose earth so that they had quite a little burrow to huddle in. Grass covered the top of the bank, and Angelique hoped it would not collapse in the rain.

Sand trickled down her neck when she leaned her head back. She wasn't really sure that this was an improvement on the rain. She was shivering hard now. François took off his jacket and wrapped it around her shoulders. The buckskin was warm in spite of being wet. She felt better right away.

"But now you will be cold, François," she protested.

"I am dry underneath and won't get too wet here. Wear it until you warm up, at least."

Angelique was grateful. Both the boys had thought to wear their jackets. Why hadn't she? She'd been in too much of a hurry to check on Michif. Never in her wildest imaginings could she have foreseen that they would be spending two nights on the prairie. She hadn't been cold the first night. It had been warm, and the fear and excitement of being captured had distracted her. Last night they'd had the campfire. But in this rain, she really regretted not bringing a jacket. Still for now, thanks to François, she was warm.

"Too bad we can't have a fire!" Joseph mumbled.

Angelique didn't say anything, though she'd been remembering the lovely coals they'd left behind at their campfire by the stream.

"Did you know, Angelique?" Joseph's spirits hadn't been dampened by the rain. "I made that fire last night?"

Angelique was impressed. He hadn't had a flint. "Very good, Joseph!" She praised. "Did you rub sticks together?" She'd never even seen him make a fire *with* a flint.

François laughed but said nothing. Joseph seemed a little crestfallen. "No," he said, "there were a few embers left from the Sioux fire. But," he said brightening, "it was almost like when you light the flint fire."

Angelique smiled. She was sure she would never feel the way she had before about Joseph, although she supposed that he would go back to being a pesky brother once they were back home. *If* they ever got back home.

"The rain is stopping," François said.

Angelique had not even noticed. She'd been letting herself imagine their fate. Three corpses lying on the prairie pecked by magpies. She was borrowing sorrow again.

"Good!" she said, trying to grin. Joseph was already out, climbing onto Gurnuy's back. She followed François. "You must take your jacket back now," she said slipping it off.

François pushed it back onto her shoulders. "Keep it on until you've dried a bit," he said, giving her a leg up onto Michif.

She gathered the reins. Michif's back was wet, but soon the warmth of him made her stop shivering again. She scanned the sky. The clouds above them had broken, and quite a bit of blue sky was showing. If the sun would just break through, they would be warm and dry in no time.

François and Pisiskees were leading the way, going back the way they had come and then heading north again.

Ahead the sky was still ominously black, and the prairie was muddy. The tracks they'd made had been almost completely erased by the rain, but François seemed to know where he was going.

Angelique wondered whether they could find their way back to Batoche if they missed the trail of the Red River carts. She had no idea how far that was.

They rode all day, with only a few stops to rest. They had nothing to eat. Angelique's mouth watered as she remembered last night's rabbit. Again she wished she'd pocketed a bit of dried pemmican. At this time of year, there were no berries. Most of the sloughs they'd passed were alkali, but at last, they came to one where they could water the horses. Around it were some reeds and cattails. Angelique remembered her mother gathering cattails. If you peeled back the tops before they ripened, they were very tasty, even if you didn't cook them.

While Michif was having his drink, Angelique managed to snap off a few. She peeled off the outside layer and began to nibble on the tender centre. It tasted fresh, and she handed some to Joseph, showing him how to peel them. On Gurnuy, he was closer to the reeds and could pick the cattails better. Soon he had picked some for himself and for François.

As they left the slough and began to ride up the next hill, François waved to them to stop.

"Do you hear hoof beats?" he asked.

It took a moment for the horses to be still so they could listen. Angelique didn't hear anything.

Suddenly Gurnuy raised his head and whinnied. Joseph tried to silence him, but then Michif and Pisiskees both began whinnying too. And then came the answering call. There were horses not far away.

"We don't know who it is," François cautioned.

"We should try to circle around and see if we can see them before they see us!" Angelique agreed.

But Joseph had kicked Gurnuy into a trot and was riding away from them. Before he could get to the top of the hill, the riders appeared. Three men.

"Papa!" Joseph had managed to get his pony into a gallop.

Angelique and François didn't hesitate. They hurried after Joseph. Angelique was filled with relief and joy at the sight of her father, but she held Michif back a little as they came closer. She would let her little brother be the one who went to Papa first. She wanted to show how much she had come to appreciate Joseph. After all, he hadn't called her "Buffalo Eyes" once during their ordeal.

CHAPTER N°. 14

To Angelique's amazement, Papa let her ride Michif the rest of the way to camp. His delight at seeing his prize horse well and safely rescued seemed to overcome everything else. For now it did not seem that he was worried about the valuable buffalo runner being spoiled. It was enough that the children were back.

When the Metis camp came in sight, people rushed to see them as word spread that they had been found. Angelique spotted her mother pushing through the crowd.

"Maman!" This time she rode ahead of the others, leaping down and running into Maman's arms. Joseph could wait his turn.

Happily, she buried her face in her mother's blouse—the familiar smell of the homespun cloth flooded her with comfort. She stayed to hide her tears. At last, she was pushed aside as Joseph crowded in to be hugged too. She and Joseph would now be pampered and fed by Maman. Angelique's mouth watered at the thought of Maman's cooking. And it would be so good to be in dry clothes again. She looked forward to curling up in her blanket in the tipi, safe and warm.

François looked as though he felt the same way. No more "adventures" for either of them for a while.

Later, as she and Joseph snuggled down to sleep, full of food and praise for their bravery, Angelique remembered the feeling of being in Maman's arms. Home. She was home already, she realized. Even though she was still a long way from their little cabin in Batoche, that settlement was home only because it was where the people who loved her lived. The Metis were settling, but family would be their true home wherever they were.

NOTES

The Metis people are descended both from the European fur traders and from the Cree, Ojibwa, and Saulteaux Natives who lived on the Canadian prairies. Their language, called Michif, evolved from a mixture of French and those Native languages. Predominantly, the language comprises Cree verbs and French nouns.

The Cree words used in the story are taken from Gerard Beaudet's *Cree-English English-Cree Dictionary*, Anne Anderson's *Metis Cree Dictionary*, and H.C.Wolfart and Freda Ahenakew's *A Student's Dictionary of Literary Plains Cree*.

page 2: *Les souliers mous ki-ka-kiskanaan. La viande pilee ki-ka-miichishunaan.*

Translation: We wear moccasins. We eat pemmican.

Note: From "La Montagne Tortue," collected by John Gosselin, in *Metis Songs: Visiting Was the Metis Way* (Regina: Gabriel Dumont Institute, 1993). Reproduced with permission.

La Montagne Tortue

John Gosselin
Lebret, Saskatchewan, 1990

La mon - tagne tor - tue ki - ki - itoh tâ - nân. En - cha - ret - te ki - ka - itotâ paso -
We are going to Turtle Mountains. We go in a cart.

nân. Les — sou-liers mous ki - ka-kis- kâ - nân. La vi - ande pi-lée ki - ka mî-ciso-nân.
We wear moccasins. We eat pemmican.

This song is sung in the Métis language called Michif, which has French nouns and Cree verbs.

page 15: *Kipaha kituun, kushon-d-shyin!*

Translation: Shut up, pig dog!

Note: *Kipaha* means "shut!" (It's the imperative form of the verb "to shut.") *Kituun* means "your mouth" (*ki-* means "your" and *tuun* means "mouth"). I imagine the last part of the expression in French would be *cochon de chien,* which, in Michif, would be *kushon-d-shyin.*

page 73: *Piiyaatak, Michif. Piiyaatak, mon buu.*

Translation: Take it easy, Michif. Take it easy, my beautiful.

Note: *Piiyaatak* (a double vowel means the vowel is long) means "Take it easy!" *Mon buu* would be the Michif pronunciation of the French *mon beau,* but the "eau" sound is actually pronounced as if it was an English "oo" sound as in "food." The Cree usually use circumflex accents to mark long vowels so it would be *Píyâtak mon bû (mon beau).*

I am grateful to Professor Robert A. Papen, Département de linguistique et de didactique des langues UQAM, Montreal, for the Michif translations used here.

BIBLIOGRAPHY

Anderson, Anne. *Metis Cree Dictionary* (Edmonton: Duval House, 1997).

Barkwell, Lawrence J., Leah Dorion, and Darren R. Prefontaine. *Resources for Metis Researchers* (Winnipeg: Gabriel Dumont Institute and Manitoba Metis Federation, 1999).

Barnholden, Michael (trans.). *Gabriel Dumont Speaks* (Vancouver: Talonbooks, 1993).

Beardy, L. (trans. by H.C. Wolfart). *Pisiskiwak Kapikisk Wecik—Talking Animals* (Winnipeg: Algonquian and Iroquois Linguistics, 1988).

Beaudet, Gerard. *Cree-English English-Cree Dictionary* (Winnipeg: Wuerz Publishing Ltd., 1995).

Charette, Guillaume (trans. by Ray Ellenwood). *Vanishing Spaces: Memoirs of Louis Goulet* (Winnipeg: Editions Bois Brules, 1976).

Erasmus, Peter. *Buffalo Days and Nights* (Saskatoon: Fifth House, 1999).

Delaney, Theresa, and Theresa Gowanlock. *Two Months in the Camp of Big Bear* (Regina: Canadian Plains Research Centre, 1999).

Dempsey, Hugh. *Firewater* (Calgary: Fifth House, 2002).

Gabriel Dumont. *Metis Songs: Visiting Was the Metis Way* (Regina: Gabriel Dumont Institute, 1993).

Hollihan, Tony. *Sitting Bull in Canada* (Edmonton: Folklore Publishing, 2001).

Lussier, Antoine S., and D. Bruce Sealey. *The Other Natives the Metis, Vol. III* (Winnipeg: Manitoba Metis Federation Press and Editions Bois Brules, 1980).

Lusty, Terrance W.J. *Metis Social-Political Movement* (Calgary: N.W. Printing, 1973).

Payment, Diane. *Batoche (1870–1910)* (Saint Boniface, Man.: Les Editions du Ble, 1983).

Ranere, Anthony J. *Fort Carlton: A Report on the Archeological Field Work* (Saskatoon: Saskatchewan Historic Sites Division, 1967).

Silver, Alfred. *Lord of the Plains* (New York: Ballantyne Books, 1990).

Stanley, George F. "Gabriel Dumont's Account of the North West Rebellion, 1885." *Canadian Historical Review* (pp. 249–269), vol. 30, no. 3, 1949.

Van Kirk, Sylvia. *Many Tender Ties* (Winnipeg: Watson & Dwyer, 1993).

Weekes, Mary (as told by Norbert Welsh). *The Last Buffalo Hunter* (Saskatoon: Fifth House, 1994).

Wolfart, H.C., and Freda Ahenakew. *A Student's Dictionary of Literary Plains Cree: Based on Contemporary Literary Texts* (Winnipeg: Department of Linguistics, University of Manitoba. Memoir 15, Algonquian and Iroquoian Linguistics, 1998).

ACKNOWLEDGMENTS

SPECIAL THANKS TO PROFESSOR ROBERT A. PAPEN FOR HIS HELP WITH THE MICHIF TRANSLATIONS. AND A BIG THANK YOU TO JOCELYN MANT FOR READING THE BOOK AND COMING UP WITH THE GREAT TITLE! I AM GRATEFUL TO MY SON SEAN LIVINGSON FOR HELPING WITH THE RESEARCH AND, OF COURSE, MANY THANKS TO MY HUSBAND, EARL GEORGAS, FOR HIS LOVE AND SUPPORT WHILE I WAS WRITING THIS BOOK.

FINALLY, I WOULD LIKE TO THANK THE CANADA COUNCIL FOR THEIR SUPPORT DURING THE RESEARCH AND WRITING OF THIS BOOK.

Dear Reader,

Welcome back to the continuing adventures of Our Canadian Girl! It's been another exciting year for us here at Penguin, publishing new stories and continuing the adventures of twelve terrrific girls. The best part of this past year, though, has been the wonderful letters we've received from readers like you, telling us your favourite Our Canadian Girl story and which parts you liked the most. Best of all, you told us which stories you would like to read, and we were amazed! There are so many remarkable stories in Canadian history. It seems that wherever we live, great stories live there too, in our towns and cities, on our rivers and mountains. Thank you so much for sharing them.

So please, stay in touch. Write letters, log on to our website, let us know what you think of Our Canadian Girl. We're listening.

Sincerely,
    Barbara Berson

Canada's

1608
Samuel de Champlain establishes the first fortified trading post at Quebec.

1759
The British defeat the French in the Battle of the Plains of Abraham.

1812
The United States declares war against Canada.

1845
The expedition of Sir John Franklin to the Arctic ends when the ship is frozen in the pack ice; the fate of its crew remains a mystery.

1869
Louis Riel leads his Metis followers in the Red River Rebellion.

1871
British Columbia joins Canada.

1755
The British expel the entire French population of Acadia (today's Maritime provinces), sending them into exile.

1776
The 13 Colonies revolt against Britain, and the Loyalists flee to Canada.

1837
Calling for responsible government, the Patriotes, following Louis-Joseph Papineau, rebel in Lower Canada; William Lyon Mackenzie leads the uprising in Upper Canada.

1867
New Brunswick, Nova Scotia and the United Province of Canada come together in Confederation to form the Dominion of Canada.

1870
Manitoba joins Canada. The Northwest Territories become an official territory of Canada.

1865
Angelique

Timeline

1885
At Craigellachie, British Columbia, the last spike is driven to complete the building of the Canadian Pacific Railway.

1898
The Yukon Territory becomes an official territory of Canada.

1914
Britain declares war on Germany, and Canada, because of its ties to Britain, is at war too.

1918
As a result of the Wartime Elections Act, the women of Canada are given the right to vote in federal elections.

1945
World War II ends conclusively with the dropping of atomic bombs on Hiroshima and Nagasaki.

1873
Prince Edward Island joins Canada.

1896
Gold is discovered on Bonanza Creek, a tributary of the Klondike River.

1905
Alberta and Saskatchewan join Canada.

1917
In the Halifax harbour, two ships collide, causing an explosion that leaves more than 1,600 dead and 9,000 injured.

1939
Canada declares war on Germany seven days after war is declared by Britain and France.

1949
Newfoundland, under the leadership of Joey Smallwood, joins Canada.

1901
Keeley

1914
Millie

1939
Ellen

Read more about Angelique
in Book One:
Buffalo Hunt

In 1865 Angelique is caught in a buffalo stampede in her first hunt with the adults.

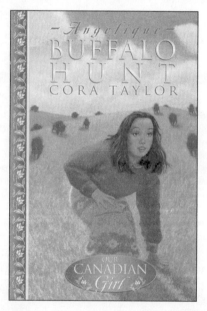

Angelique's third book is due to be published in fall 2005!